# The Balloon Launch

ISBN 0-7696-4220-9

50395

9 780769 642208

EAN

Text Copyright © Evans Brothers Ltd. 2005. Illustration
Copyright © Evans Brothers Ltd. 2005. First published by
Evans Brothers Limited, 2A Portman Mansions, Chiltern
Street, London W1U 6NR, United Kingdom. This edition
published under license from Zero to Ten Limited. All rights
reserved. Printed in China. This edition published in 2005 by
Gingham Dog Press, an imprint of School Specialty
Publishing, a member of the School Specialty Family.

Library of Congress-in-Publication Data is on file with the publisher.

Send all inquiries to:
School Specialty Publishing
8720 Orion Place
Columbus, OH  43240-2111

ISBN 0-7696-4220-9

1 2 3 4 5 6 7 8 9 10 EVN 10 09 08 07 06 05

# The Balloon Launch

By Helen Bird

Illustrated by Simona Dimitri

Columbus, Ohio

There was a balloon launch
at Mike's school.
Every student got a balloon.

5

Each balloon had a note
tied to it.
Mike's note read:

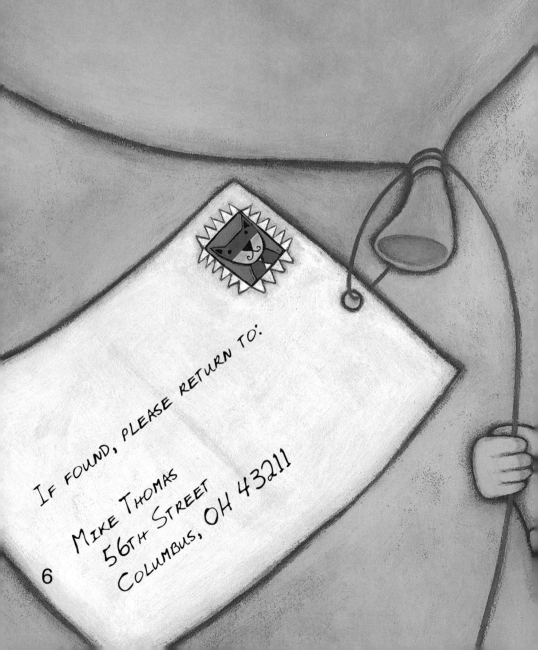

IF FOUND, PLEASE RETURN TO:

MIKE THOMAS
56TH STREET
COLUMBUS, OH 43211

6

"I hope my balloon goes far!"
said Mike.

8

9

It was time to launch the balloons.
"One, two, three, let go!"
said the teacher.
The balloons flew high into the air.

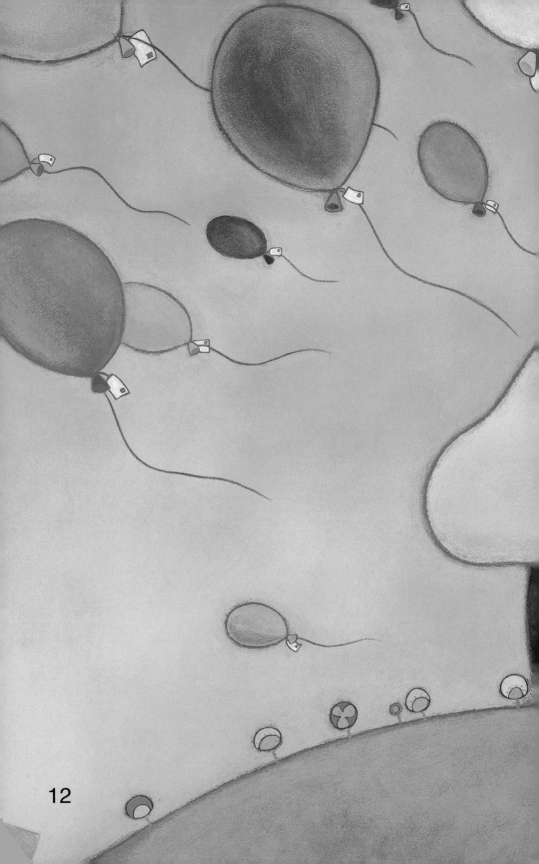

All except Mike's balloon.

His balloon didn't go very far
or very high.

His balloon floated down.
It got stuck on a truck.

The truck drove out of town.

It drove up into the hills.

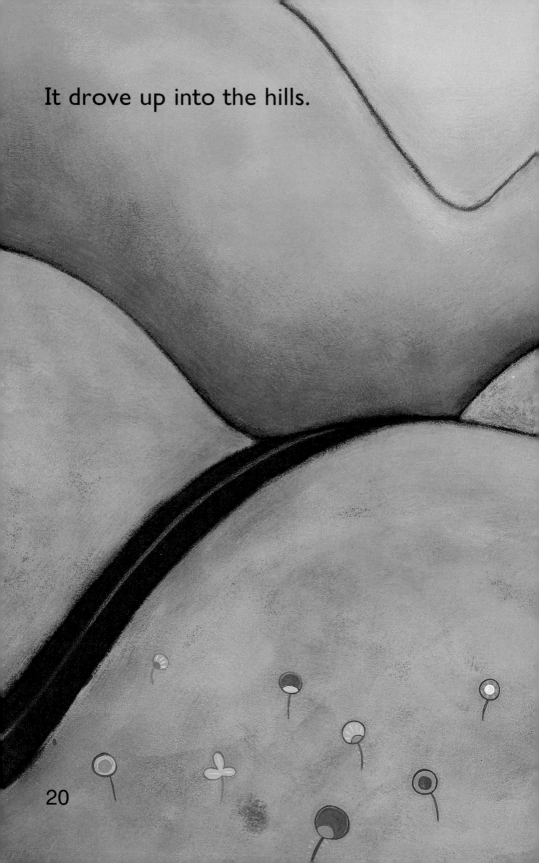

It drove all through
the night.

The truck even crossed the ocean!

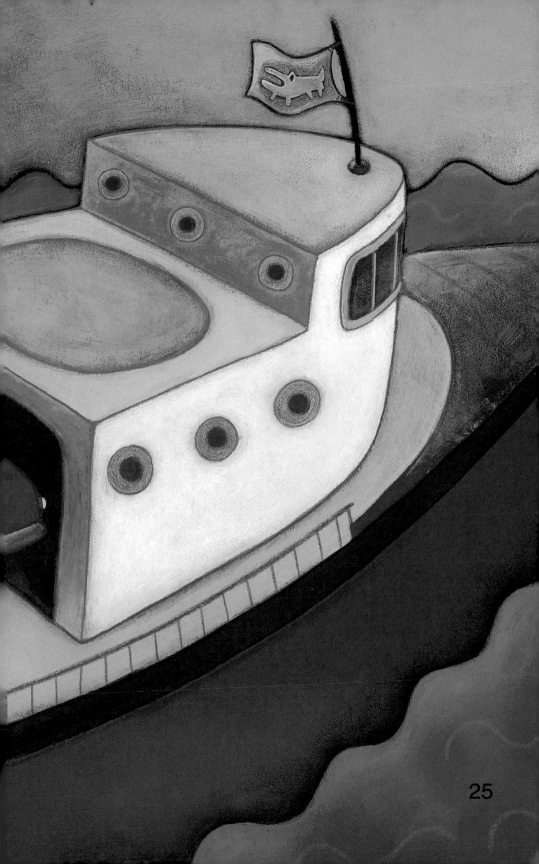

The truck driver found the balloon.
*Hmm*, he thought. *I will mail this.*

Mike forgot about his balloon.
He didn't think it had gone very far.

But it went farther than everyone else's!

27, Via Manzoni
Milan, Italy
1-20121

If found, please return to:

Mike Thomas
56th Street
Columbus, OH 43211

## Words I Know

| | |
|---|---|
| down | one |
| every | three |
| far | two |
| found | went |

## Think About It!

1. What did the note on Mike's balloon say?
2. How do you think Mike felt after the balloon launch? How do you think he felt at the end of the story?
3. Name all of the places that the truck traveled.
4. How far do you think Mike's balloon traveled?
5. At the end of the story, whose balloon traveled the farthest?

## The Story and You

1. Do you think this story could really happen? Why or why not?
2. Pretend that you are Mike's balloon. Describe all of the things you saw while you were traveling.